Numbers Parade

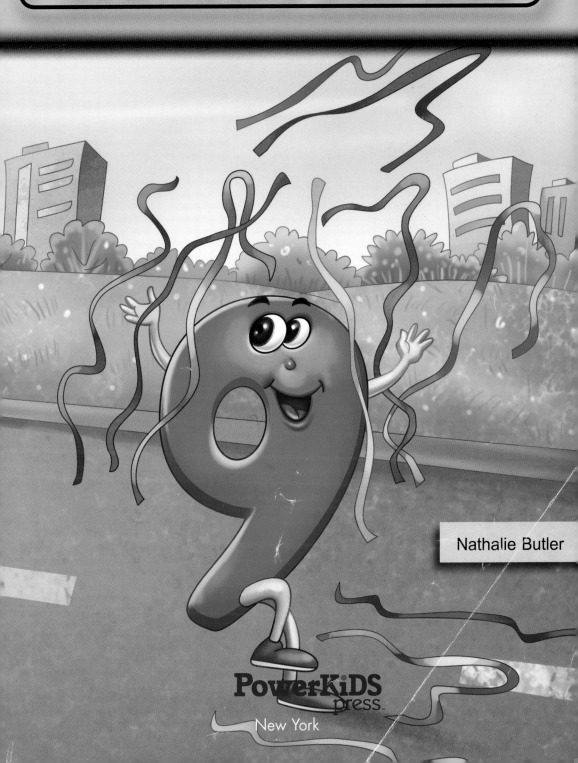

Nathalie Butler

PowerKiDS press

New York

Published in 2018 by The Rosen Publishing Group, Inc.
29 East 21st Street, New York, NY 10010

First Edition

Book Design: Brian Garvey
Illustrations by Continuum Content Solutions

Cataloging-in-Publication Data
Names: Butler, Nathalie.
Title: Numbers parade / Nathalie Butler.
Description: New York : PowerKids Press, 2018. | Series: Learning with stories | Includes index.
Identifiers: ISBN 9781508162339 (pbk.) | ISBN 9781508162353 (library bound) | ISBN 9781508162346 (6 pack) | ISBN 9781508162360 (ebook)
Subjects: LCSH: Numbers–Juvenile fiction. | Counting–Juvenile fiction.
Classification: LCC PZ7.N863 2018 | DDC [E]–dc23

CPSIA Compliance Information: Batch #BS17PK: For further information contact Rosen Publishing, New York, New York at 1-800-237-9932

Manufactured in the United States of America

Contents

You can always count on numbers. One through Nine are oh so fine.

NUMBERS PARADE

For showing price, they're
also nice. See the people,
big and small?
Numbers let you count
them all!

5

**Say hello to the number One–
the very first number under the sun.
One leads the way in the numbers
parade.**

One's all alone, but not for long.
The other numbers are coming along.

Two follows One, but not too close.
Today he's second best.
He doesn't care
because, you see,
he's still ahead of the rest.

After Two comes Three, you see.
As playful as can be.

Three rides a "trike,"
a kind of bike.
Let's count the wheels—
one, two, THREE!

There's more. There's Four.
The family of Four joins in.
Two by two, mom, dad,
and kids.

And look, there's Five!
He's giving us high-fives—up high!

Six has a belly big and round.
He beats it like a drum.

Pound! Pound! Pound!
Pound! Pound! Pound!
Hear that happy sound!

Lucky Seven rides on a float
made out of wood and
shaped like a boat.

Sometimes people mix up Seven with One.

Seven is actually
bigger, though.
Seven comes later,
and has farther to go.

The number Eight is next in line.
Right after Seven,
right before Nine.

Eight twirls a rope like
cowboys do,
and even makes it loop-the-loop.

Number Nine doesn't mind
being last in line.
Get ready for change when you see
Nine.

Because after number Nine is when two numbers follow— making Ten.

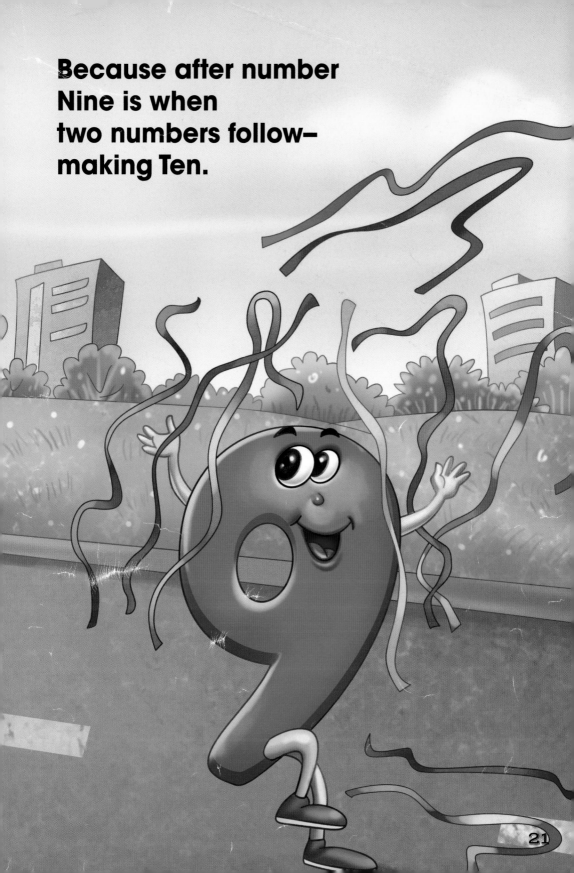

The Numbers Parade has
come to an end.
Thank you for watching,
my friends.

Words to Know

float

parade

trike

Index

B
boat, 16

C
cowboy, 18

D
drum, 15

F
family, 12

P
parade, 6, 22

S
sun, 6

**Although they are through,
remember, please do—
you can always count on numbers!**